SHARE A STORY

One, Two, Flea!

Introduction

One of the best ways you can help
your children learn and learn to read
is to share books with them. Here's why:

• They get to know the **sounds**, **rhythms** and **words**
used in the way we write. This is different from how we
talk, so hearing stories helps children learn how to read.

• They think about the **feelings** of the characters
in the book. This helps them as they go about
their own lives with other people.

• They think about the **ideas** in the book. This helps
them to understand the world.

• Sharing books and listening to what your children
say about them shows your children that you care
about them, you care about what they think
and who they are.

Michael Rosen

Michael Rosen
Writer and Poet
Children's Laureate (2007-9)

First published 1986 by Walker Books Ltd
87 Vauxhall Walk, London SE11 5HJ

This edition published 2011

2 4 6 8 10 9 7 5 3 1

Text © 1986 Allan Ahlberg
Illustrations © 1986 Colin McNaughton
Concluding notes © CLPE 2011

This book has been typeset in Caslon 540
Printed in China

British Library Cataloguing in Publication Data:
a catalogue record for this book is available from the British Library

ISBN 978-1-4063-3513-2

www.walker.co.uk

One, Two, Flea!

Written by
Allan Ahlberg

Illustrated by
Colin McNaughton

WALKER BOOKS
AND SUBSIDIARIES
LONDON · BOSTON · SYDNEY · AUCKLAND

One, two, three,
mother finds a flea,
puts it in the teapot
to make a cup of tea.

The flea jumps out,
mother gives a shout,
in comes father
with his shirt hanging out.

Four, five, six,
father's in a fix,

wants to get the billy goat
to hatch a few chicks.

The chicks hatch out,
father gives a shout,

in comes granny
with her hair sticking out.

Seven, eight, nine,
granny's doing fine,
scrubs all the children
and pegs them on the line.

The line gives way,
granny shouts "Hey!"
"Wow!" shout the children…

and they all run away.

Tiny Tim

I have a little brother,
his name is Tiny Tim,
I put him in the bath-tub
to teach him how to swim.

He drinks up all the water,
he eats up all the soap,
he goes to bed
with a bubble in his throat.

In comes the doctor,
in comes the nurse,

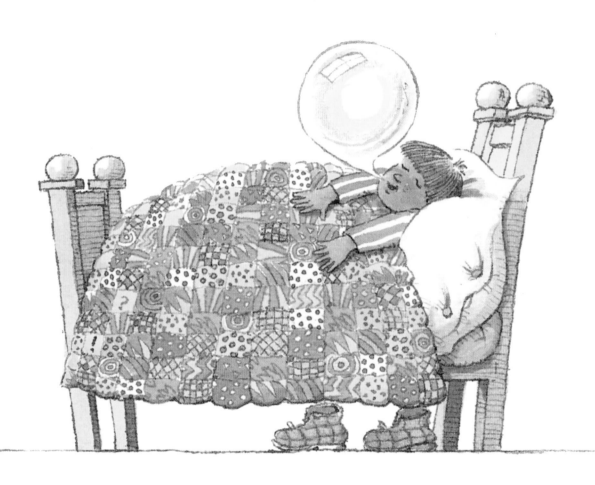

in comes the lady
with the alligator purse.

"Dead!" says the doctor.
"Dead!" says the nurse.
"Dead!" says the lady
with the alligator purse.

But he isn't!

POP!

I have a little sister,
her name is Lorelei,
I push her up the chimney
to teach her how to fly.

She runs about the roof-tops,
she chases all the crows,
she goes to bed
with a feather up her nose.

In comes the doctor,
in comes the nurse,

in comes the lady
with the alligator purse.

"Dead!" says the doctor.
"Dead!" says the nurse.
"Dead!" says the lady
with the alligator purse.

But she isn't!

Sharing Stories

Sharing stories together is a pleasurable way
to help children learn to read and enjoy books.
Reading stories aloud and encouraging
children to talk about the pictures and join in
with parts of the story they know well are
good ways to build their interest in books.
They will want to share their favourite books
again and again. This is an important part
of becoming a successful reader.

One, Two, Flea! presents two funny rhymes from the winning author-illustrator team of Allan Ahlberg and Colin McNaughton. Here are some ways you can share this book:

• With two rhymes featuring the same family in different situations, this book offers children an early introduction to the idea of chapters.

• Both rhymes encourage children to have a go at joining in the reading. In **One, Two, Flea!** they can follow the counting rhyme pattern; in **Tiny Tim** the strong repetition supports their reading and there's an amusing alternative version about a little sister to grab their interest.

• If children get stuck on a word you can help them to guess what it might be by using the pictures, the meaning of the story and the first letter of the word. You can also help them to break down the word into syllables or chunks, e.g. stick-ing. If they're really stuck, just give them the word and carry on reading to keep it an enjoyable experience.

• Together you can look at the patterns in the rhyme to encourage children's interest in how words are written down. You can make rhyme cards and play a "matching pairs" game. It can include rhyming words from the book and rhymes with family names, e.g. Polly-jolly, Sue-blue, Ben-ten.

SHARE A STORY
A First Reading Programme
From Pre-school to School

Beginnings – 2 years+

Look Out, Suzy Goose — Petr Horáček
Walking Through the Jungle — Julie Lacome — Introduced by Michael Rosen
Hello, Goodbye — David Lloyd, Louise Voce — Introduced by Michael Rosen
Penny Dale — TEN IN THE BED — Introduced by Michael Rosen
THIS IS THE BEAR — Sarah Hayes, Helen Craig — Introduced by Michael Rosen
The Big Wide-Mouthed Frog — Ana Martín Larrañaga — Introduced by Michael Rosen

Early Steps – 3 years+

A New House for Mouse — Petr Horáček — Introduced by Michael Rosen
The Train Ride — June Crebbin, Stephen Lambert — Introduced by Michael Rosen
THE OTHER DAY I MET A BEAR — Russell Ayto — Introduced by Michael Rosen
Jane Chapman — Old MacDonald Had a Farm — Introduced by Michael Rosen
The Tiger and the Jackal — Vivian French, Alison Bartlett — Introduced by Michael Rosen
Zed's Bread — Mick Manning, Brita Granström — Introduced by Michael Rosen

Next Steps – 4 years+

The Hairy Toe — Daniel Postgate — Introduced by Michael Rosen
The True Story of Humpty Dumpty — Sarah Hayes, Charlotte Voake — Introduced by Michael Rosen
BEANS ON TOAST — Paul Dowling — Introduced by Michael Rosen
Over in the Meadow — A Counting Rhyme — Louise Voce — Introduced by Michael Rosen
Polly Dunbar — Dog Blue — Introduced by Michael Rosen
Introduced by Michael Rosen — Night-night, Knight And Other Poems — Michael Rosen, Sue Heap

Taking Off – 5 years+

"Have You Seen the Crocodile?" — Colin West — Introduced by Michael Rosen
HANDA'S SURPRISE — Eileen Browne — Introduced by Michael Rosen
The Ravenous Beast — Niamh Sharkey — Introduced by Michael Rosen
Allan Ahlberg, Colin McNaughton — One, Two, Flea! — Introduced by Michael Rosen
Nick Sharratt — Dinosaurs' Day Out — Introduced by Michael Rosen
The Old Woman and the Red Pumpkin — Betsy Bang, Rachel Merriman — Introduced by Michael Rosen

Sharing the best books makes the best readers

WALKER BOOKS

www.walker.co.uk